POSIES OF GRATITUDE
TO SUSAN —M. C.

TO JESSICA —A. O.

IMPRINT
A part of Macmillan Publishing Group, LLC
120 Broadway, New York, NY 10271

ABOUT THIS BOOK
The art in this book was created with marker, pencil, brush
pen, charcoal, cut paper, and Photoshop. The text was set in
New Caledonia and the display type is Lydian. The book was
edited by Erin Stein and designed by Natalie C. Sousa. The
production was supervised by Raymond Ernesto Colón, and the
production editor was Ilana Worrell.

Library of Congress Cataloging-in-Publication Data is available.

ISBN 978-1-250-31481-9 (hardcover)

Our books may be purchased in bulk for promotional, educational,
or business use. Please contact your local bookseller or the Macmillan
Corporate and Premium Sales Department at
(800) 221-7945 ext. 5442 or by email at
MacmillanSpecialMarkets@macmillan.com.

Imprint logo designed by Amanda Spielman

First edition, 2020

10 9 8 7 6 5 4 3 2 1

mackids.com

This book is like a flower—
if you didn't plant it,
don't pick it for your own bouquet.
Leave it for others to enjoy.

THE BEAR'S GARDEN

MARCIE COLLEEN

ILLUSTRATED BY ALISON OLIVER

{Imprint}
New York

IN THE BIG, BUSTLING CITY, all the people were busy.
They rushed up and down the street without seeing that
some buildings needed paint, that some buildings were
empty, that some buildings were gone.

But in one girl's imagination,
the city was a place to grow,
a place to play,

a place to love.

She could always find
beauty around her.

One night, the girl's imagination
spilled onto the sidewalk,
rolled across the street,
and sprouted.

"A baby garden!"
When she spotted the seedling, she introduced
herself with a "How do you do?" and a garden party.

And that's how it
went, day after day.

No matter how fierce the
sun or how swift the wind,
the little girl watched
over the seedling.

"I believe in you,"
she whispered every
morning and every night.

More seedlings soon grew.

People rushing by began to slow down.
First, with a tip of the hat or a nod of the head.
People stopped to smile or say hello to the little
girl with the tiny green friends.

There came a time when the girl had
to leave for a while.
    Without her care and without her love,
she knew the plants would wither.

She wanted to bring
the garden with her,
but it wasn't possible.

She thought maybe she could
whisper "I believe in you"
from far away, but she didn't
have enough string.

She tried employing a pigeon,
but it was clearly not trained.

If the little girl could not take care of the garden,
someone else would have to.

She filled her bear with cuddles and snuggles
and stuffed him full of hope.

She locked button-eyes with him and whispered into his ear, "This is a very special mission. Watch the garden until I get back."

She kissed him on top of his head
and left him to do his job.

From miles away, the girl imagined the garden was blooming.

A place to play.

A place to love.

And it was.

AUTHOR'S NOTE

The Pacific Street Brooklyn Bear's Community Garden was founded in 1985 and named for a teddy bear that was sitting in the weeds. On this neglected corner in Brooklyn, New York, the community came together to launch a beautification project that has continued for more than twenty-five years.

Although no one knows how the bear got there, it is the inspiration for this story.

Today Brooklyn is home to numerous community gardens and each provides a place to grow, a place to play, and a place to love. But most important, a place to imagine what can be.